BAKED BETRAYAL

RAISED AND GLAZED COZY MYSTERIES,
BOOK 31

EMMA AINSLEY

SUMMER PRESCOTT BOOKS PUBLISHING

CHAPTER ONE

"Why are you still hanging around here?" Orson Hawley grumbled at Maggie Mission as she refilled his coffee mug. He was seated in the same spot he had occupied at Dogwood Donuts since before it was so named, back when Maggie's great-aunt, Marjorie Getz, was the proprietor. The table was situated front and center in the dining room and as the de facto head of the old timers, Orson's place was at the head of the table.

"What are you talking about?" Maggie asked. "It's only nine o'clock in the morning. Where else would I be today?"

"Well, you ought to be on your honeymoon," Orson muttered. "As a matter of fact, you should have gone on your honeymoon months ago. Sometimes I don't know how that husband of yours has the patience to put up with this."

"To put up with what? What does Brett have to put up with from me that I don't already put up with from him?" Maggie asked. "You do know there have been quite a few things going on around here for both of us, right? It's been a little bit difficult to get away together."

"Well, neither of you are spring chickens," Orson said. "As they used to say back in my day, you need to make hay while the sun shines. There's no time like the present. Do you need another trite idiom to get you motivated to go on your honeymoon?"

"No, no, I think I've got it," Maggie said. She held the coffee carafe in front of her and sighed. "Your point isn't lost on me. I know we need to get together and get out of town for a while."

"It isn't like you don't have expert help back here to take care of everything while you're gone," Orson continued. "As a matter of fact, it might do everyone some good for you to get out of town for a while."

"What is that supposed to mean?" Maggie asked. "You really think the staff would do better without me around?"

"That's not what I'm saying at all, and you know it." Orson sighed. "I think we both know everyone could use a change of pace, and everyone could use a break from each other."

Maggie stood staring at him for a long moment. She waited for him to elaborate on what he'd said, but Orson turned his attention back to his coffee mug and ignored her. "So that's it? You have nothing more to say after all of that?"

"Once again, I think you get the point." Orson smiled. "Now, run along back to the kitchen and let me know when the fresh cinnamon rolls are finished. I want one hot and fresh as soon as they're ready."

"Yes, sir," Maggie said with a salute. She turned on her heels and headed behind the counter. She replaced the pot on the coffee maker as she walked past and pushed through the swinging door into the kitchen. She threw her hands up and shook her head as she entered.

"What's that all about?" Ruby Cobb, her best friend and business partner, asked from her position at the prep table.

"Orson," Maggie said as she began to wash her hands.

"What about him?" Ruby asked. "Or maybe I should say, what's the matter now?"

Maggie put her arms down at her side and marched over to the baker's table. She uncovered the rising cinnamon roll dough and punched it repeatedly with her fist. "Oh, that man," she said. "He just had the nerve to lecture me on how important it is for Brett and me to actually get away and take our honeymoon together. As if I don't already know that!"

"Well, it has been a few months," Ruby said.

"Not you too," Maggie gasped. "Although his second point was how it would be beneficial to everyone else around here if I was gone for a while. Do you share in that sentiment as well?"

Ruby laughed and shook her head. "Leave it to Orson," she said.

"Leave what to Orson?"

"Leave it to him to state the obvious," Ruby said. "Look, I'm not saying that we've all spent too much time together lately, but I do think we've all had a rather rough year. It would do us well to spend some time apart."

"What is this?" Maggie asked. "Some sort of a mutiny? Does everyone feel this way?"

"Does everyone feel what way?" Naomi Gardner asked as she entered the kitchen.

Maggie turned to face her. "Does everyone think that I need to get out of town for everyone else's sake?"

Naomi glanced nervously at Ruby. "Well, it isn't exactly like that."

"Then what is it exactly?" Maggie asked.

"We just think you need a break. You've been very stressed lately, and it shows," Naomi said.

"Not that any one of us blames you," Ruby interjected quickly. "I mean, we've all been around and seen what this past year has been like. It hasn't been easy for any of us, but you and Brett are newlyweds. It's clear that all of this has put a strain on you. I have a feeling that's put a strain on him as well."

"So, what is it you want me to do? Demand that Brett takes leave from his job right when they are the most shorthanded they've been in five years?" Maggie asked. "You do know that the main reason we haven't gone anywhere is because of what's going on at the Sheriff's Department right now, right?"

Ruby nodded. "Of course. We understand things are difficult for him at work as well, but Orson isn't wrong. Both of you would benefit from some time away. Sometimes, you just have to grab the bull by the horns and make it happen."

Maggie folded her arms over her dusty apron. "What do you suggest I do?"

"Grab the bull by the horns," Myra Sawyer

Macklin said from behind her. Maggie turned around and frowned. "Not you, too."

"Oh, yeah," Myra said. "Me, too."

"It's a conspiracy," Maggie complained to Brett later that night. They were seated in the backyard on the wicker loveseat she had purchased shortly after their wedding. She rested her head on his shoulder as they gazed at the sunset.

"What's a conspiracy?" Brett asked her.

"Everyone at work thinks you and I need to get out of town as fast as possible," she said. "Not for the reasons you might think, either. Apparently, me getting away for a while is to benefit everyone else, not just the two of us."

Brett shook his head and laughed. "There must be something in the air," he said.

"Why do you say that?"

"Let's just say your employees aren't the only people who think that way," he said. "Even my secretary has weighed in on the fact that we need to get away."

Maggie exhaled slowly. She squeezed his hand and looked up at him. "Does that mean we're grumpy? Do you think that's what they're trying to say?"

Brett nodded. "I think it's very likely, and to be

honest with you, sweetheart, I'm not sure I disagree. I have to admit things have been getting to me a little bit lately. I know they've been getting to you, too."

"How do you know that?"

"Because when you sleep, you toss and turn and mumble things under your breath about the donut shop," he said. "That is, when you do get any rest at all."

"I suppose you're right," Maggie said. "I should say, I suppose everyone else is right, too."

"So, what are we going to do about it?"

"I guess we're going to make reservations somewhere and get away for a week," Maggie said. "Either that or I suppose we could take an early retirement. Maybe then everyone else will be happy."

"I don't think it's that bad," Brett said. "I have to admit that getting away for a little while sounds like heaven to me."

"I suppose we better get on the laptop and make some reservations, then," Maggie said. "What are you thinking? Mountaintop retreat? Seaside adventure?"

"What about a week in a cabin in the Smoky Mountains?" Brett draped his arms around her shoulders. "You're not the only one that hasn't been able to sleep. A few nights ago, I started looking at cabins by a river in Tennessee. I even checked to see when the available dates were. They had openings for the rest of the month."

"It sounds like all we have to do is just make the reservations," Maggie said. "Could it really be that easy?"

"I think it really can be that easy, if we put our minds to it." Brett stood up and stretched his arms above his head. He yawned loudly then place both hands on his hips. "Let's go inside and make the reservations before we can think twice about it."

"What about work? What about you taking time away from the Sheriff's Department?" Maggie asked. "Don't you need to give them some advanced warning?"

"I'm not saying we'll leave tomorrow, but I think a few days' notice will be more than enough. Why don't I make the reservations while you call Ruby and let her know?"

Maggie followed him inside through the back door. As they stood in the kitchen, she found herself grinning ear to ear. "I can't believe we're going to do this," she said. "I mean, I really can't believe we're about to do this."

"That smile tells me this is something we should have done a long time ago," Brett said.

CHAPTER TWO

Maggie arrived at work early the next morning. She tied her apron around her back and immediately began mixing the cake donut batter for the donut machine. As soon as the batter was in the hopper, she started the large stand mixer for the cinnamon roll dough. Once the dough was ready and set aside to rise, she got to work on the scone batter.

By the time Ruby's key turned in the back door, Maggie had already completed most of the morning's tasks. She'd even removed a bushel of apples from the cooler and began grating them for Ruby's famous apple slaw.

"Wow. You were busy this morning," Ruby said.

"I decided to get here a little early to see what I could get done." Maggie smiled. "Besides, everyone's been working so hard around here, I thought maybe I'd give everyone a little bit of a lighter morning."

Ruby laughed out loud and shook her head. She pulled her clean apron off the hook outside the storage room and tied it around her waist. "Spill it," she said. "I know you have something to tell me. It's written all over your face and I can tell by the change in your attitude that there's something you're happy about."

"I have no idea what you're referring to," Maggie said.

"Oh, yes, you do." Ruby grinned. "Out with it. Now."

Maggie turned her back to her best friend and pretended to ignore her while she began to roll out her first batch of cinnamon rolls. "Well, there is this one thing," she said. "I was going to text you last night, but it was rather late when we finally settled on something. Brett and I made reservations for a mountain retreat in Tennessee. I took your advice, and we are actually going on our honeymoon."

Ruby whooped and headed straight for her with open arms. She gathered Maggie up in a hug and squeezed tightly. "I am so happy for the two of you," she said. "When do you leave?"

"Not for a few more days," Maggie said. "Brett

had to give a little bit of notice at work, even though they seem just as excited to get rid of him as you all have been to get rid of me."

"Oh, knock it off." Ruby laughed. "No one around here is eager to get rid of you."

"I know," Maggie admitted. "I'm just giving you a hard time. I did take a lot of what you said yesterday to heart, though. It is about time we got away."

A second later, there was a knock on the back door. Ruby moved to answer it. "Pardon me, excuse me," Naomi said as she sailed into the kitchen. Her arms were filled with canvas shopping bags.

"What is all this?" Maggie asked. She rushed over to assist Naomi with the groceries.

"I hope you don't mind," Naomi gushed. "I saw this fantastic new donut variety last night and I wanted to try it. I hope that's okay."

"Did you really just ask me if it's okay for you to try a unique donut flavor?" Maggie chuckled. "Of course, it's okay. In fact, I wish we had more ideas from you and Myra."

"So, what's the mystery flavor?" Ruby asked. She poked around in the grocery bags for a moment. "I see some rather interesting things in here." She pulled out a small bag of jalapeño peppers.

"Are you making a jalapeño flavored donut?" Maggie asked.

"Yes, but it isn't going to be like you think. I had one of these at the mall last night and I begged the woman for the recipe. She wouldn't give it to me, so I had to go home and put it together myself. I hope you guys like it."

"There's only one way to find out," Ruby said. "Here, let's give you some room to get busy. I'll take over frosting the cake donuts in between my prep work for lunch so you can concentrate on your new donut flavor."

"Thank you," Naomi said. "I planned to work on things in between my other duties."

"Nonsense," Maggie said. "Why don't you get a few dozen whipped up and we'll give them out to the customers today and see what they have to say?"

Naomi smiled and got to work. Maggie watched as she mixed the sweet dough they typically used for yeast donuts. She was a little shocked when Naomi added a small amount of jalapeño juice to the batter. Naomi then cut out four-inch squares from the dough and left them on a pan to rise. When the donuts had risen high enough, she moved them to the deep fryer. She fried them in batches, then mixed several jars of strawberry preserves and jalapeño jelly together for the filling.

"I'm not sure what to think about this," Ruby said an hour later. The first strawberry jalapeño donuts were cooling on a rack while Naomi mixed a basic cream cheese frosting for the top.

"Good morning," Myra said just before eight. "What is that smell? There is definitely something a little different in the air in here today."

"Naomi has graced us with her very own invention of a strawberry jalapeño donut," Maggie announced.

"Oh, are these like the ones they had at the mall last night?" Myra asked. She rushed to the cooling rack and picked up a donut. Without warning she bit into it and closed her eyes. "No, these are even better!"

"Do you really like them?" Naomi beamed at Myra.

"I absolutely love these," Myra said with her mouth full of donut. She turned to Maggie. "You guys simply have to add these to the menu."

Ruby glanced at Maggie and shrugged. She moved to the cooling rack and plucked two more donuts off the tray. "I guess the two of us better try these before anyone else does," she said and bit into it. Maggie accepted the other donut from her and took a bite herself.

"That is the most unexpected taste," Maggie said. "I honestly don't know what I was expecting, but it wasn't this."

"Is that good or bad?" Naomi asked nervously.

"Oh, it's good." Maggie nodded. "Very, very good." Ruby said nothing but nodded enthusiastically.

"You better set one of those aside for Orson," Maggie said.

"That might not go too well," Ruby said. "You know how cantankerous he can be."

"Speaking of cantankerous," Maggie chimed in. "The two of you will be happy to know that I will be going away."

Naomi glanced at Myra. "What are you talking about?" she asked.

"The two lovebirds are finally going to take off on their honeymoon," Ruby said.

CHAPTER THREE

Maggie sat upright in the seat. She gazed out the windows at the sun coming up and the mist lifting off the mountains in the distance. "Where are we?" she asked in a whisper. The mountains outside her window seemed to demand reverence in her voice.

"We're east of Wildwood," Brett said. He picked up a foam coffee cup from the console and handed it to her. "You were sound asleep when I stopped for gas. I hope it's still hot."

Maggie carefully pressed the coffee cup to her lips and sipped. "It's just right," she said. "Thanks for getting me some coffee. Sorry I slept through the drive."

"It's okay, honey," Brett said. "Your job starts a lot earlier in the morning than mine does."

"You're being pretty generous, but thank you," Maggie said. "How much longer until we get to the campground?"

"About another hour," Brett said with a yawn. "Do you need to stop anywhere?"

"I'm okay for now." Maggie turned back to the window and stared at the view. Living in the Ozarks was a treat. She loved her hills and loved the rocky forests around them, but there was something special about these mountains, something that took her breath away.

"It's alright," Brett said. "You can say it."

"I can say what?"

"You can say that I picked the perfect place to go on our honeymoon," Brett said. "I know it seems a little premature, but I think it's pretty clear that I've already done quite well with my choice."

"I have to admit that it's beautiful." Maggie chuckled. "But let's reserve judgment until the end of the week. I mean, I'm not going to give you the satisfaction of telling you that you were right if I get chased by a bear when I'm trying to use the restroom."

"You're not going to get chased by a bear when you're using the restroom," Brett said. "We're staying indoors. I rented us a cabin."

"But otherwise, I might get chased by a bear," Maggie said. "Is that what you're saying?"

"Now you're just putting words in my mouth," Brett said.

Maggie turned the radio up. She sipped her coffee and listened to the downhome country tunes as they drove down the highway. In no time, Brett was turning off the road onto a gravel driveway into the campground.

"This place comes up on you kind of fast, doesn't it?" Maggie waited until Brett parked the truck and then stepped outside. She stretched her arms over her head and walked a few paces to get her legs under her again. It felt good to stretch after so many hours in the truck.

"I think we need to check in down there." Brett pointed. "That looks like the place on the website."

"Which one do you think is our cabin?" Maggie asked. As they walked, she gazed at the long row of small log cabins among the trees. She could hear the river rushing somewhere in the distance though she couldn't see it through the dense forest.

"I think we're down on the other end," Brett said. "Here we go. Here's the office." He pulled on a door handle made from a small branch and waited as she stepped inside.

A moment later, Maggie followed him down a narrow hall. The place was dimly lit. She looked around for signs of anyone inside the cabin. "Hello," she said.

"Oh, hold on," a voice called out in the distance. Maggie was sure it belonged to a woman, and an older one at that. A second later, her assumptions were confirmed. She heard the woman's boots across the wooden floor before she saw her. When she stepped into view, Maggie wondered for a moment if they had stumbled across the property of a famous country music singer. "No, I am not her. Everyone thinks I am, but I'm not. I'm just a local girl from the hills. I can't carry a tune in a bucket either."

"I suppose you hear that all the time," Brett said. He reached his hand out and shook the woman's hand. "My name is Brett Mission, and this is my wife, Maggie. We have reservations through the tenth."

The woman broke into a smile. "You sure do," she said. "Follow me this way and I'll get you your room key." Her slim figure passed quickly through the long hallway and turned to the right. She was dressed in dark wash jeans and a button-up shirt. If she wasn't a country music star, she easily could have passed for one. Her long, dark hair hung loose around her shoulders. A thick band of silver hair framed her face on either side.

"I don't think I got your name," Maggie said when they caught up with the woman. She turned into what appeared to be the dining room of the log cabin and took a seat behind a wooden desk.

"That's probably because I haven't had a chance to tell you," she said. "My name is Darlene Sloane. I am the sole proprietor of this property, the receptionist, and too often, the maid. It's a pleasure to meet you."

"You run this place by yourself?" Maggie asked. She was impressed, and not just because of the woman's age.

"Is it that hard to believe that an oldie like me could keep this together?" Darlene asked with a chuckle.

Maggie shook her head. "Not at all."

"My wife is a business owner herself," Brett explained. "Even though she has a terrific team of people to help her, she's had times when being a business owner has been a lot to deal with."

"He's right," Maggie said. "I run a donut shop, but that seems like nothing compared to keeping a place like this going. How long have you been here?"

"Oh, let me see now," Darlene said. She stared at

the ceiling for a moment. "I opened this place all the way back in 1986. I've been on my own here since."

"Wow," Brett said simply.

"Yup. All by my lonesome," Darlene said. "It's not as bad as it sounds. I've had a great life. How many women my age get to wake up and look at those mountains every morning? Trust me, I've enjoyed every minute of it."

Maggie jumped when a clap of thunder startled her. "I wasn't aware the weather was supposed to turn," she said, gripping the shirt under her throat.

"It's iffy one way or the other," Darlene said. "In this area, weather tends to go one way or the other. Either good or bad. We often don't know which way until it happens upon us."

"If you don't mind, I'd like to get settled into our cabin before the rain hits," Brett said. "Thanks again for everything."

"It was nice to meet you," Maggie said. She followed Brett back down the dimly lit hallway toward the entrance. When she opened the door to step outside, she was met with a gust of cool air. "Dang. The temperature has really dropped."

"Yeah, and quickly." Brett hesitated at the door of the truck. "You know, with all this dirt, I'm not so sure I want to drive all the way down there if it's going to rain. Do you think we can carry all of our luggage to the cabin?"

"I only have one bag and my purse," Maggie said. "I think we can handle it. Besides, I'd rather not get stuck in case we decide we want to go somewhere later."

Brett grinned. "Oh, sweetheart, we won't be going anywhere tonight," he said. "Why do you think I insisted on bringing a big cooler? We have dinner for tonight and breakfast in the morning. Once we get settled in the cabin and build a fire, I have no intention of leaving anywhere for at least the next 18 hours."

Maggie cast a sideways grin at him. "Okay, it sounds like you have everything planned out for a romantic evening," she said. "Does that mean you're going to do the cooking, too?"

"You'd better believe it," Brett said. He walked around to the back of the pickup and lowered the tailgate. Moments later, they walked down the footpath to the second to the last cabin on the end.

Maggie felt her heart racing as they neared the cabin. She hadn't felt so much excitement in a long time. Here they were, under the shadow of the gorgeous mountains and the pine trees and there was nothing to do but sit and relax. Even the rainstorm brewing couldn't dampen her spirits.

Brett hefted the large cooler on wheels up onto the covered porch and left it outside. Maggie was the first inside the cabin. "How gorgeous," was all she could think to say when she stepped inside. The inside of the small cabin was a mixture of rustic elegance and country coziness. She ran her hand over the lace table covering on the antique buffet table inside the front door.

"The bedroom is that way, if you want to drop off your bag," Brett said when he walked in behind her.

"I'm in love," Maggie breathed.

"I should hope so," Brett quipped. "Have you ever met a more loving husband in your life?"

Maggie rolled her eyes and carried her luggage into the bedroom. She was excited to see the quilt covered four poster bed and the fireplace in the corner. She set her bag on the floor and fell backward into the fluffy bed.

"I think I'll just pass out here for a little while," she said when Brett came in the room. "Please don't wake me until it's time to leave."

"Why don't you just hang out in here while I get dinner underway?"

"No, no. I'll help you with dinner," Maggie said, raising up from the bed.

"Nope," Brett said. "You are not allowed to help with dinner tonight. The only thing you are permitted to do is sit on the porch and watch the rain while I grill the steaks."

"Oh, that's silly," Maggie said. "At least let me make the mashed potatoes."

Brett shook his head. "Not happening," he said. Maggie followed orders and took a seat on the cozy front porch. She covered herself with a knitted throw blanket from inside and watched as he prepared dinner. Less than an hour later, they were seated side by side watching the rain as it fell on the mountains.

Maggie enjoyed a glass of wine after dinner and then another one before she followed Brett sleepily across the small log cabin and into bed for the night. Rain drummed softly on the roof as they fell asleep. Maggie found herself sighing deeply and cuddling further under the handmade quilt on top of the bed. Just before she fell completely asleep, she wondered if there had ever been such a perfect moment.

Right before three in the morning, Maggie woke with a start. Somewhere in the night, she had heard a woman scream. She sat up and looked around the room. Embers glowed in the fireplace from the fire

Brett had built just before they fell asleep. She listened for a moment, then closed her eyes, sure she had been dreaming. She looked over at Brett who was gently snoring and laid her head back on her pillow.

She was just about to fall asleep again when she heard someone on the front porch. Seconds later someone wrapped loudly on the front door. Brett sat up straight and put his legs over the side of the bed. "Stay here," he commanded. He padded quietly across the room and into the living area. Maggie watched as he looked carefully through the curtains to see who was on the front porch.

"It's a woman," he called back to her.

"Please, someone," the woman wailed on the other side of the door. "Someone help me!"

Brett threw the front door open and stared at the woman. "What is going on out here?" he asked. "Why do you need help?"

"My friend," the woman cried. "He's gone!"

"Your friend left you?" Brett stepped back and folded his arms over his chest. Even in the darkness, Maggie could tell he was frustrated by his tone of voice.

The woman shook her head. "No, no. You don't understand," she said. "My friend, my companion. He's gone. Dead. He died."

Immediately, Brett's body language changed. He dropped his arms to his sides and glanced back at Maggie, who was now standing a few feet away, watching and waiting. "Call the police, and then call Darlene in the office." He grabbed his jacket from the hook by the door and headed out into the rainy night with the woman.

CHAPTER FOUR

Maggie ran to her phone and dialed the police. She punched 911 into the keypad and held the phone to her ear. Nothing happened. She checked the screen again and ended the call. When she tried it the second time, the phone ended the call itself. She checked her signal and realized she had no service.

"Now what?" she mumbled to herself in the darkness. She glanced at the front door and ran for her shoes. She pulled her sweater on over her nightgown and headed out into the night behind Brett. Lights burned in the cabin to the left, the last cabin at the end of the row. She burst onto the covered front porch and gazed inside. Brett stood with his back to her. The woman was next to him. Her shoulders quaked as she sobbed.

"I can't call the police," Maggie blurted. "I'm sorry, but there's no signal. I have no cell service."

"Stay here with her then," Brett said. "I'm going to run up to the office and see if I can use the phone in there."

"Brett," Maggie said quietly as he passed her. "Are we, I mean, should we worry that this was intentional?"

"Yes, we should," Brett said. "If anything happens while I'm gone, you scream as loud as you possibly can."

"Okay," Maggie replied. "Hurry back. And Brett, be careful."

She stepped up next to the older woman and draped her arm around her shoulders. The woman leaned into her and sobbed harder. Maggie held on for a moment then swallowed hard.

"Okay, okay," she said softly. "I know this sounds harsh, but you need to tell me what happened. Can you remember?"

The woman pushed back away from her and rubbed her hand over her eyes. She shook her head for a moment then burst into fresh tears. "I'm sorry," she said. She inhaled deeply and dried her eyes again. "Okay. I heard something in the kitchen, and I reached over to see if Dale was still beside me in the bed. When I realized he was gone, I got up and walked into the kitchen to see if he was alright. He has a chronic heart condition and sometimes has to get up in the middle of the night and take medication. It's one of the reasons we don't get away on vacation very often. This time, his doctor gave him the go ahead, so we drove up here." She bowed her head and sobbed again.

"What happened when you came out here, from the bedroom, I mean?" Maggie asked.

Her question prompted the woman to take another deep breath and stop her crying. "I found him, there on the floor," she said. "I rushed to his side and felt for a pulse, but there was nothing, just nothing."

"Is that when you screamed?"

The woman shook her head. "No, I screamed when I saw someone standing there behind the curtains." She looked up at the long, lacy sheers that covered the front window. "As soon as I screamed, whoever it was ran outside into the night."

Maggie noticed for the first time that there were no electric lights burning. Kerosene lanterns lit up the room. "Did you light these?"

The woman nodded. "I tried to turn on the lights, but nothing happened when I flipped the switch," she said.

Maggie opened the screen door and looked down the long row of cabins. Porch lights burned on most of the other cabins. The electricity hadn't gone out everywhere. She closed the door and stepped back inside. Clearly, someone had cut the power to the cabin.

"Are you sure there was someone there?" she asked. "I know that question seems strange, but sometimes when we're afraid or upset our mind invents things. My husband is a county sheriff back home in Missouri. Are you absolutely sure that you saw someone in here?"

"Absolutely sure," the woman said soberly. "I swear on my life I did. They took off and ran as soon as I screamed."

"Do you know which way they went?" Maggie asked.

"Straight out into the night," the woman said.

Maggie jumped when she heard footsteps on the front porch. A second later, Brett appeared at the front door. "I can't get anyone at the office." He looked over at the woman. "Do you know where Darlene, the owner, sleeps?"

The woman nodded. "She lives in the cabin where the office is located. She's lived there since she took over this place."

"Do you know Darlene Sloane well?" Maggie asked her.

"Yes. She's my older sister. I'm Charlene."

Maggie moved closer to the body. It was difficult to see much in the low light and the shadows that danced because of the flickering flames, but she could tell from the dark puddle that surrounded the head the man had been struck, hard.

"This man, Dale, is he your husband?"

Charlene shook her head. She reached out for Maggie's arm and fell into her. Her eyes rolled back in her head. "Brett!" Maggie shouted. "Help me, please." Brett took the woman from her arms and laid her down gently on the sofa.

"I wish this rain would stop," he said. "I'm starting to worry that it may be difficult to get emergency vehicles down here."

"Right now, we need to focus on finding Darlene," Maggie said. "If this is her sister, she may know what to do next. I don't remember, did she have a landline in the office?"

Brett nodded. "I think I ought to head back up to her place again," he said. "Maybe if I beat a little harder on the door she'll actually wake up."

"I don't think we should separate again," Maggie said. "I'm not sure if you heard what Charlene had to say or not, but that scream came when she looked up and saw someone standing in the shadows behind the curtain. This man was murdered."

"I know he was," Brett said quietly. "I'm not in any hurry to leave you here by yourself, but in this case, I think we're running out of options. I would rather you be in here where you can lock the doors than be out there running around in the darkness with all this rain. I highly doubt whoever did this is going to come back for a second round."

"I hope you're right," Maggie said.

Before he had a chance to go looking for her again, Darlene appeared at the open front door. "Is something going on here?" She trudged inside the room and chunks of mud fell from her rubber boots. "Oh my gosh! What's wrong with my sister?"

"Miss Sloane," Brett said quietly. "If you take a look in the kitchen, you're going to see what's wrong."

Darlene's eyes ventured from her sister, who was still passed out cold on the couch, to the body lying on the floor in the shadows in the kitchen. Her hand flew to her mouth, and she dropped her head. "His heart finally gave out," she said. "Didn't it? I knew this trip was going to be too much for him."

"It wasn't his heart, Miss Sloane," Brett said.

"The best I can tell, someone hit him over the head with a blunt object. The pool of blood around him indicates that he died from blunt force trauma. Of course, the local coroner will have to make that pronouncement."

"How do you know all of this?" Darlene asked. "Are you some kind of a doctor?"

Brett shook his head. "No, not at all," he said. "I'm a county sheriff. You might say I've had experience with these things before."

"Where exactly is it you're from again?" Darlene asked.

"Southern Missouri," Brett said. "We live in the Ozarks."

Darlene smiled slightly and crossed the room to her sister's side. Maggie was a little surprised that she tracked mud so far into the beautiful log cabin, but supposed it was the least of the woman's worries at the moment.

"We need to be able to call the police, ma'am," Maggie said. "I can't get cell signal anywhere."

"They wouldn't be able to get in here anyway." Darlene placed her hand softly on her sister's forehead and brushed the hair out of her eyes. "I'm afraid the river has flooded up the road quite a bit and we are at its mercy until this storm is over."

"Wait a minute," Brett said. "What are you saying? Isn't there another way out of here?"

Darlene fixed her gaze on her sister. She shook her head and looked up slightly. "There isn't. Even if they wanted to, the police couldn't get here. No one is coming or going from here until the flooding recedes."

CHAPTER FIVE

"Don't you have a working phone in your place?" Maggie asked next. She felt herself growing irritated with Darlene's lack of motivation, or whatever it was. Her sister needed medical attention. The man on the floor needed to be moved, and there was evidence all over the place.

"I do have a phone in my house, but it stopped working an hour ago," Darlene said. "Like I told you before, we're just going to have to wait until the floodwaters recede to get any help."

"Well, the sun will be up in a few hours," Brett said. "We need to get your sister out of here. Can you try to rouse her? Then maybe we can move her to your house for the time being. Meanwhile, everyone needs to leave so I can take some crime scene photos at the very least."

"No, no," Darlene said. "I don't want you to do anything. I will stay right here with my sister. If you want to do something, get him out of here."

"I'm afraid that's not how it works," Brett said quietly. "As a law enforcement officer, I know how things are supposed to be done, ma'am. This crime scene has already been contaminated, and we don't need any more of that to happen. I'm afraid I have to insist that you help me move your sister to your cabin."

"He's right," Maggie said. She tried her best to sound comforting and understanding. "If there's ever going to be any chance of figuring out who did this, we have to do things very carefully. Brett here knows how things need to be done. Why don't I help you with your sister?"

Darlene said nothing more but moved to the couch and began shaking her by the shoulder. "Charlene, honey, it's your sister," she said. "Come on now and wake up. We need to get you out of here."

Charlene moved around for a moment, but her eyes didn't open. Darlene knelt by her and shook her again, this time patting her face vigorously. Still, Charlene's eyes did not open.

"Let me try," Brett said. He stood over the couch and folded his arms. "I'm going to need you to leave these premises, right now. Charlene? You need to get up and go with your sister." His deep voice boomed through the small cabin. Charlene's eyes popped open. She looked up and stared at Brett.

"Well, that worked," Darlene said. "Come on. Let's get you out of here."

"No, no," Charlene argued. "I don't want to leave! I don't want to leave Dale here by himself."

"You have to leave," Brett said. "Like I told your sister, if the police can't get here because of the flooding, then it's up to me as a law enforcement professional to secure the scene. You need to go. I know that sounds harsh, but if we're ever going to find who is responsible for this, the best thing we can do is conduct as thorough of an investigation as is possible under the circumstances."

"I hate to say it, but he's right," Darlene said.

"I can't go out there," Charlene argued again. "It's raining cats and dogs. In fact, I think the rain is coming down harder now."

Maggie looked down and noted that the woman's shoes were still on her feet. "I wish you had some boots to wear. Either way, let's just get this over with."

"I agree with you there," Darlene said. She pulled her sister to her feet and ushered her quickly to the front door. Charlene continued to argue the entire way up the steep path in the rain to her sister's house.

Maggie found herself on the opposite side of Charlene. The woman leaned her weight heavily on her as they fought their way through the sticky mud and up the path to the opening of the campground. More than once she thought she was going to land face first in the mud. By the time she left Darlene and Charlene outside of the cabin door, her legs burned from the strain.

She wrapped her soaking wet sweater around her middle and ducked her head as she headed back down the path toward her cabin. Maggie was almost at the bottom of the hill when she felt her feet fly out from under her. She landed hard on her back and as soon as she hit the ground, she felt the wet sticky mud in her hair.

"Oh, dear." An older man appeared suddenly over her. In the darkness, Maggie only saw a hand extending toward her. She grabbed on and allowed herself to be pulled to her feet. Two sets of arms reached out and steadied her.

"Are you okay? We heard some noise and thought we would come out and see what was wrong," the woman standing next to him said. "I'm Sadie John-son. This is my husband, Tom. Do you know what's going on out here?"

Maggie nodded and brushed the mud out of her hair. "Thank you for your help," she said. "We're staying in Cabin 11. I'm afraid there was an accident in Cabin 12. My husband is down there right now dealing with it."

"What kind of an accident?" Tom demanded. "Those are our friends in Cabin 12."

"Let's head down towards my cabin, and I'll explain everything when we get to the front porch out of the rain."

Sadie stood on the other side of her husband and hooked her arm through his. Without a word, Tom slipped his free arm around Maggie's shoulders and guided her to the cabin. They said nothing until they stepped up onto the front porch out of the rain.

"Has anyone called the police or an ambulance?" Tom asked. "I mean, I would assume that if there's been an accident involving a woman screaming, well, I would think someone would have called for help by now."

Maggie immediately thought it was an odd question, but it was an odd night. "According to Darlene Sloane, there's too much flash flooding in the area," she said. "As a matter of fact, the phone lines are down and there is no cell service. So, we couldn't call to get help even if there was a way for them to get to us."

"Forgive me for being too blunt, but why is your husband in the cabin?" Sadie asked. "What does he have to do with any of this?"

"My husband, Brett, is a trained law enforcement officer," Maggie said. "I guess you could say he's doing his best to preserve the crime scene until the real authorities can get here. We are on vacation from southern Missouri where he is a county sheriff."

"Ah, I see," Tom said. "I'm starting to think something happened to one of our friends. Since you were just coming back from Darlene's cabin, I'm going to assume that person was Dale. Am I right?"

Maggie nodded and shivered in the cold wind. "I am so sorry to have to tell you this, but Dale was found dead on the kitchen floor. I am so sorry. Would you like to sit down?"

Sadie gasped and her husband draped his arm around her. "Dale was her stepbrother," he said quietly. "I'm afraid this is a lot for her to take in. I think I'll just walk her back to our cabin. We're in Cabin 9. Will you please let us know if your husband discovers anything? Or if the authorities are able to get through?"

"Of course, I will," Maggie said. "Again, I'm so sorry for having to break the news to you this way. I had no idea you were friends of Charlene and Dale. Please accept my condolences."

Maggie watched the older couple head back toward their own cabin. As soon as they were out of sight, she took her boots off outside and padded back inside the warmth of her own rental. She peeled off her wet sweater and immediately went to the kitchen window where she could see the cabin next door. Brett was over there all alone. She knew he could take care of himself, but there was a part of her that worried the killer might come back and find him there by himself.

She spotted his shadow passing a window and reached for the light switch next to the sink. She flicked the light on and off for a moment and smiled when his face appeared in the glass. She waved at him and gave him the signal that she was okay. He nodded his head and gestured at her to stay there. At least, that's what she interpreted his hand gesture to mean. She nodded her head and mouthed, "I love you." Brett smiled and mouthed the words back to her then turned from the window.

Maggie headed immediately to the bedroom and pulled fresh clothes out of her bag. She turned on the hottest shower she could stand and stepped into the tub. It took a full twenty minutes to get the sticky mud out of her hair. When she emerged, she wrapped the towel around her and dressed in front of the fireplace.

As soon as her hair was dry enough, she headed into the kitchen where she began a pot of coffee on the old stove. She filled the top of the percolator basket and set it inside the antique coffee maker. The coffee would be strong, but it might be just what Brett needed when he came back, whenever that was.

Maggie didn't have to wait too long. Brett appeared at the front door an hour after her shower. His hair was wet, but he was otherwise fine. He took his boots off outside and headed straight for the small couch.

"I smell coffee," he said.

"I assumed it might be a long night," Maggie said. "I'm afraid I can't make you a cinnamon latte, but I can make it good and strong and black."

"That sounds like just what the doctor ordered." He shook his head and leaned back with his eyes closed. "I wish there was a doctor around. I find it unsettling that someone else hasn't pronounced the victim dead."

"Brett, do you think there's any chance..." Maggie began.

"No, he had been gone for a little while," Brett said. "Of course, without a forensic team here, it's very hard to pinpoint exactly how long, but the blood around his head was already sticky. That didn't just happen."

"Well, then, what do you make of what Charlene said?" Maggie asked. "Do you think she was lying?"

"No, not at all," Brett said. He accepted the hot coffee from Maggie and thanked her. "I don't think Charlene was lying, but I do think she was in shock."

CHAPTER SIX

Brett stayed awake and looked out for as long as he could keep his eyes open. He told Maggie that he was determined not to let anyone near the cabin. The closer it was to the dawn, the harder that would be, he said.

Maggie did her best to stay awake alongside him, but somewhere just before five in the morning, she awoke to find herself wrapped in a blanket with her head on a pillow. She looked up to see Brett standing by the front door gazing toward the last cabin.

"Did you get any sleep?" She stood and raised her arms above her head.

Brett turned to her and frowned. "No, I didn't," he said. "I can tell you one thing, though. It sure knows how to rain in Tennessee."

"Has it let up at all?" Maggie stood up and padded across the room and into the kitchen. She turned the fire back on under the coffee pot and waited for it to boil.

"Not really," Brett said. "If anything, it's gotten worse. I'm beginning to worry about that river. I don't know where we're going to go if it starts to flood."

"I hadn't thought of that," Maggie said. "I kept thinking about having a way to get in. I hadn't really thought about the way out."

"Hopefully, we're high enough up that the river doesn't pose any real threat to us," Brett said. He turned around and gazed back outside. "The sun will be up soon."

"I imagine we're going to be flooded with questions as soon as it is," Maggie said. "No pun intended."

"Did you say you met another couple last night on the way back from Darlene's cabin?" Brett stepped away from the front door for the first time since she had been awake.

Maggie nodded. "It was an older man and woman. Tom and Sadie Johnson. Sadie is Dale's stepsister."

"So, they are here on vacation with Charlene and Dale?" Brett asked.

"I would assume that's the case, but they never actually told me that. I wonder how Sadie is doing this morning. She was pretty upset last night, understandably so."

"We'll find out soon enough," Brett said. "I'm going to have to go down there and have a talk with both of them. I need to find out what they know or what they might have seen last night."

"Do you want me to go with you?" Maggie asked. She picked up his coffee mug from the table next to the sofa and refilled it with hot coffee.

Brett nodded as he took the cup from her. "I think that would be a good idea," he said. "For one thing, I'd like to have you standing outside on the porch where you can keep an eye on the cabin. Secondly, it might be good to have someone else there to witness the conversation."

"You should take your cell phone with you," Maggie said.

"Why?" Brett asked. "Do you think we might have signal now?"

"I have no idea," Maggie said. "But you have a voice recorder on your cell phone."

Brett's face broke into a grin. "I knew there was a reason I kept you around," he said. He crossed the room and wrapped her in a big hug. "That and the donuts. You know I'm a sucker for donuts."

Maggie hugged him back. "At least I know I'm good to keep around for something," she said. "Do you think we should go up to Darlene's cabin and check in on them? I wonder how they did last night?"

"It's still raining pretty hard out there," Brett said. He released her from his embrace. "Before we do anything, I think I'm going to have a look around the cabin and see if I can't find some rain gear or something."

"That's not a bad idea," Maggie said. "I think there's a utility room in the back. I'll start looking there." She left Brett in the living room and walked through the cabin to the small laundry room. She opened the small closet and looked through a few of the garments hanging up that they might be able to use. She checked the shelf above and found a small umbrella. It wasn't much, but it was better than nothing.

Maggie noticed that the room continued around the corner. She walked past the washer and dryer and turned to the left, surprised to see a windowed door to the outside. The electrical panel was situated on the wall just before the door. She moved the mini blinds back and looked outside. The back of the cabin was just feet from the tree line. She could see the river beyond it.

"Hey, what are you doing back here?" Brett asked.

"Honey, come here and look at this," Maggie said. She led him to the back door and pushed the blinds back for him to peer out. "I wonder if all the cabins are the same."

Brett stepped up and looked outside. "Because if they are, this is probably where the killer accessed the electrical panel." He sighed. "Something about this just doesn't make any sense."

"I found an umbrella in the closet," Maggie said. "I think you need to go over there and check out the back of their cabin."

"I think you're right." Brett held out his hand for the umbrella. "Are you going to be all right here by yourself?"

"I'll be fine," she said. "Do you still plan to go and talk to the Johnsons?"

"As soon as I get back." Brett turned and headed back through the cabin to the front door. He hesitated for a moment and then called back to Maggie. "Why don't you just go with me?"

"Are you sure?" Maggie asked. "I mean, of course I'll go with you. But is something wrong?"

Brett shook his head. "Not exactly. I just think I'd like it better if you were with me. As soon as we're finished at Cabin 12, we'll walk down and talk to the Johnsons."

Maggie smiled. "Lead the way, Sheriff," she said.

CHAPTER SEVEN

Maggie waited on the front porch of Cabin 12 while Brett went inside. She held the umbrella and turned to watch the rainfall. After several moments, she ventured off the porch to walk around the side of the cabin. She sloshed her way through the sticky mud and rounded the back of the cabin. The small utility room jutted out of the otherwise square structure. Maggie stood at the corner and looked toward trees.

"That's weird," she said to herself. Despite the gray skies overhead, there was enough light to see the ground surrounding the cabin. She held on tight and gazed deep into the woods.

The river roared in the distance. Maggie thought about what Brett had said earlier about the water rising from the river and wondered if they were in any real danger. She turned to head back to the front of the cabin when Brett popped around the side.

"What are you doing?" he called out to her.

"Just looking at the back of the cabin." Maggie clung tightly to the cabin and made her way back toward the front. The rain continued to pelt the umbrella as she carefully walked to meet Brett. He reached for her and practically pulled her to him when she was close enough. She glided over the mud like she would over the water on a pair of skis.

"What were you doing back there?" Brett asked. "I figured you were still on the front porch staying out of the rain."

"I guess I don't have the sense to stay out of it." Maggie chuckled. "I wanted to see what the back looked like."

"Did you find anything?"

"No," she said. "That's the weird thing."

"What do you mean? What is so weird about not finding anything?"

"I guess I just assumed that the perpetrator had come through the back to attack Dale, but there was nothing back there. Nothing at all. No footprints, no tracks of any kind."

Brett eyed her carefully. "That is strange," he said. "Well, since I hadn't gotten around to checking out back just yet, I suppose it's kind of you to have done it for me."

"Not hardly," she said. "That wasn't my intention, but I do find it strange that there are no tracks back there."

"It could mean that the rain washed them away," Brett said.

"Maybe," Maggie said, then looked out at the ground surrounding the porch. "But our tracks from earlier are still here, and it is raining harder now than it was last night when Charlene knocked on our door."

"That's very true," Brett said. "I'm not sure what any of this means yet. For now, I think we ought to go and pay the Johnsons a visit."

"Then maybe we can get back to the cabin and dry off for a little while," Maggie said. She hooked her arm through Brett's elbow and waited for him to step off of the porch again.

He sighed and gazed at her for a moment. "I'm sorry, Maggie," he said softly.

"Sorry for what?" Maggie asked.

"That our honeymoon turned into a murder mystery," he said. "This is not what I had planned for us this week."

Maggie shrugged. She gazed up at the gray sky

and shook her head. "I don't think either of us had this planned, but what are we going to do? Like you said, you're the only law enforcement officer around here. We can't just ignore that a man was killed last night."

"I wish I knew what to do about the body," he said as they walked. "It's going to have to be moved, and soon. I think we need to find a tarp or something to wrap him in."

"Maybe we should talk to Sadie about that," Maggie suggested. "After all, if he is her stepbrother, I suppose that makes her the closest thing to the next of kin we have available."

"Good point," Brett said. "To be honest, that's a good way into a conversation with her. Maybe we should check and see if there is finally cell signal."

"On it." Maggie handed Brett the umbrella and pulled her phone out of her back pocket. She tapped the screen and checked. "Still nothing. I don't even have a single bar."

"That really stinks," he said when they reached the cabin.

Maggie followed Brett up to the small front porch, and waited while he knocked on the front door.

"Oh, Maggie, right?" Tom greeted her.

"That's right, and this is my husband, Brett

Mission," she said. "Like I said before, he is the county sheriff back home in Dogwood Mountain County, Missouri."

Tom held the front door open for them. "Nice to meet you, Sheriff." He looked over his shoulder. "Sadie, that nice lady from earlier and her husband are here. I think they want to speak to us about your brother."

Sadie made her way into the living room and took a seat on the small couch. Under the overhead light, Maggie could see signs of very little sleep. She was an older lady, perhaps in her seventies, but the circumstances of the day made her look even older.

"How are you?" Maggie asked her.

"As well as could be expected, given the circumstances," Sadie said. "Please, have a seat."

Brett and Maggie took their seats on the other side of the room.

"Now, Sheriff, what is it we can do for you?" Tom asked.

Brett cleared his throat and sat forward. "As I'm sure you are aware, these are rather unusual circumstances we find ourselves in," he began. "Like my wife told you, I am an active sheriff back home in Missouri, and since we're unable to reach local law enforcement, and they are unable to reach us, I'm doing the best I can to investigate your brother's death."

"We thank you for that," Sadie said.

"I have a few rather indelicate questions to ask you," Brett said. "And an unusual request."

"Why don't you start with the request?" Tom suggested.

"Okay, then," Brett said with a sigh. "Without the ability to get an ambulance or coroner here, something needs to be done with Dale. I'm sorry, what is his last name? I don't think Charlene ever told us."

"Bushman, Dale Bushman." Sadie nodded her head after she said his name. "His mama married my dad when we were just kids. We came up together. I can't tell you how hard this hits."

"I'm so sorry to hear that," Brett said. "This is a part of my job that I really hate. I need to deal with, well, Dale's body, and it's a little tricky right now without the coroner here to take care of things."

"I grew up on a farm in Georgia," Sadie said. "My daddy raised enough livestock that I know what needs to happen, Sheriff. What exactly is it you are asking?"

Brett sighed. Maggie looked over at him and her heart melted a little bit. She hated how hard this must be on him. She also hated how their honeymoon had turned into this terrible situation for everyone but wasn't going to admit that to Brett right now.

"I'm going to ask Darlene for a tarp, and Tom, if you feel up to it, I may need your help. I think it would be fitting if a member of the family took part in this. We need to find someplace cold for Dale until the sheriff can get here."

"Do they even know yet?" Sadie asked. "I mean, has anyone been able to inform the police? Local police, I mean."

Brett shook his head. "No, and that's why all of this is so tricky," he said. "I'm trying to do everything I can to preserve the integrity of this investigation until they can get here. The last thing I want to do is put this in jeopardy and somehow make it so that the killer gets away entirely. I don't want to do that to your family."

Sadie nodded. "I understand that, and thank you," she said. "Now, in the beginning, you said that there were some questions you needed to ask."

"I did indeed," Brett said. "I need to ask you how close you were to your brother."

"Stepbrother," Tom corrected.

Brett smiled. "You're right," he said. "My apologies. Exactly how close were you to your stepbrother? You said the two of you grew up together."

"We did," Sadie said. "I was nine and he was eleven when our parents got married. We didn't live together all the time, but we spent most of our summers and plenty of other holidays and vacations together on my dad's farm. After the divorce, my mother moved us to the city, but my favorite times were always back at home on the farm. Dale and I were thick when we were kids. He was my protector when I was a teenage girl going out on dates and such."

"This has to be so hard for you," Maggie said.

"It isn't very easy, but I know that there's a job that needs to be done," Sadie said. "What else do you need to know?"

"I need to know if you know of anyone that might have wanted to hurt him," Brett said bluntly.

Sadie gazed at her husband for a moment. Maggie thought she saw Tom give a curt shake of his head to his wife before she answered. "Honestly, aside from the fling he's had with Charlene all these years, I can't think of any reason someone would want to do him harm."

"Fling? Charlene and your brother were having an affair?" Brett set upright on the couch. Maggie could tell that this last revelation had gotten his attention.

"Since they were very young. I'm sorry, Sadie, I

know you don't like to admit that to yourself, but they've both been married for a very long time to other people." Tom turned his attention back to Brett. "They've carried on with this affair for decades. It was a shock to me that my wife agreed to come here for this weekend."

"What was this weekend supposed to be?" Maggie asked.

"Dale is retiring from the automotive business after five decades," Sadie said with a slight grin. "He booked this vacation far away from home because he wanted to celebrate with the people who would really understand what his life had been like. It is a real triumph for him that he's able to retire after all these years."

"And why is that?" Brett asked. "Is there any special reason why his retirement is different?"

Tom nodded. "Dale has beat cancer, three times," he said. Sadie sobbed and covered her mouth. She stood and walked to the other side of the room. "It's something of a miracle that he lasted this long, long enough to retire."

"Why not celebrate with his wife and the rest of his family?" Brett asked.

Sadie dropped her arms to her sides. "You would have to know his wife, Hilda," she said. "As much as

I disapprove of my stepbrother's extramarital activities, it's an open secret that his wife is something of a shrew."

"That's a little harsh," Tom said. "Plenty of people have difficult marriages, but not everyone steps outside of their vows."

"You really didn't care for your brother-in-law, did you?" Brett asked.

"No, I didn't, but before you ask that million-dollar question, I never would have hurt him. I may not have approved of what he did, but I'm not a violent man. I hold no hate in my heart for him, and I was here with my wife all night long."

Maggie wondered what was going through Brett's head at that moment. Was Tom a suspect? Looking at him, she wondered how he would have managed to trudge through the night in the mud and rain just to hurt Dale. He was by no means a weakling, but he was a man of advanced age. It didn't seem very likely that he could have done it.

"Okay, thank you for your honesty," Brett said. He turned to Sadie. "I presume you will back his story up?"

"Are you really asking me if my husband murdered my brother?" Sadie snapped. "I understand you have a job to do here, Sheriff, but these questions are getting tiresome."

"Alright then." Brett stood up. "Tom? Do you feel up to helping me with the body?"

Tom nodded. "We might as well get it over with," he said. "I think there's a large walk-in freezer in one of the cabins up front. Once in a while, the place is used as an event venue. I'm sure we can make arrangements for him there."

"Wonderful," Brett said. "Sadie, I apologize for putting you through this. I hope you understand this is just part of what must be done. Would you like for my wife to stay with you for a little while?"

Sadie shook her head and managed a slight smile. "Thank you, but no," she said. "I think I will avail myself to a long nap. I'll be fine while Tom helps you."

Maggie stood up next to Brett. "I'll be in our cabin while the men take care of your brother," she said. "If you need anything, you know where to find me."

Sadie nodded and left the room without another word.

"Give me a few minutes to see to my wife, Sheriff," Tom said. "I'll meet you on the front porch of Dale's cabin."

"Good enough." Brett led Maggie out the front door. They picked up the umbrella and headed back to their own cabin.

"Well, what do you think?" Maggie asked as soon as they were out of earshot.

Brett shook his head again. "I think there's a lot more going on here than what we realize," he said. "The real question is, does any of it have to do with Dale's death?"

Maggie stopped and looked at him. "You don't buy Tom's alibi, do you?" she asked.

"I actually do," he said. "I'm not sure Tom is capable of committing murder, but I think there are a lot of other things I don't know about yet. I have many doubts, and I don't know what direction to look in first."

CHAPTER EIGHT

"I think I'm going to head back up the hill and check on Darlene and Charlene," Maggie announced.

Brett hesitated and looked up the hill for a moment. "Are you sure you want to make that trek again? If you want to, how about you just go back to the cabin and wait for me? As soon as I'm finished dealing with Dale's body, I'll go with you."

Maggie shook her head. "I think I should go up now. As far as I know, neither you nor Tom Johnson have alerted her to the fact that you might be bringing a dead body to a different cabin of hers."

"That is a very good point," Brett said. "Yes, please inform Darlene that we will be headed her way shortly."

"Do you want me to wait for you up there?"

"Why don't you wait for me, and we can come back down the hill together?" he said. "I might need your help getting Tom back to his cabin." Maggie was unsure whether the last part was a joke or not, but she planned to wait for him anyway.

Brett walked to the right while she walked up the path toward the top of the hill. Rain continued to fall, and Maggie managed to stay on the grass well enough to keep her footing as she trekked up the hill. When she reached the top, she looked back toward the long line of cabins. She noticed for the first time that the tree line was closer to the last three cabins than the rest of them. In fact, the cabins in the middle had a bit of a backyard that the other cabins didn't.

Before she made her way to Darlene's, she turned to look at the river on the other side of the forest. The sound of the rushing water had grown to an almost deafening level, but she couldn't tell from her vantage point how far out from the banks the river may have gotten.

It dawned on her that without the use of her cell phone or even a landline, it may be difficult to hear any new flood warnings or weather bulletins. Surely, however, if Darlene had a radio she should be able to hear any news.

Maggie stepped up onto the wrap-around porch and walked toward the front door. She knocked loudly and waited for Darlene to answer. After half a minute, she raised her hand to knock again. The door opened just as her fist struck it. Darlene stood on the other side of the door. Her face was red and puffy, and her eyes showed clear signs that she had been crying hard.

"Darlene," Maggie gasped. "Are you all right?"

Darlene swallowed hard before she opened her mouth to speak. "Have you seen my sister? Have you seen Charlene this morning?"

Immediately Maggie shook her head. "I haven't seen her anywhere," she said. "Have you checked the entire house?"

Darlene stepped out of the way to allow her to come inside. She nodded her head and burst into a fresh round of tears. Unlike the day before, she was dressed in a pair of soft flannel pajamas with her long hair pulled back. She looked much less like a hardened cowgirl and more like a fragile older woman.

"We were up late into the night." Darlene wiped her eyes with the back of her hands. "Charlene was talking about everything. She said Dale's wife had been on to them for years. I'm assuming you know my sister and Dale were having an affair."

Maggie nodded. "I just came from Sadie Johnson's cabin," she said. "Tom and Sadie filled me and my husband in on everything."

Darlene stared blankly at her for a moment. Maggie wondered if the woman had been drinking the night before, and if the effects of the alcohol still had an influence on her. "Charlene told me she thought this was going to be her last weekend ever alone with Dale. She was so sad when we went to bed last night, but I couldn't keep my eyes open any longer. I shouldn't have left her! I should have stayed by her side all night long."

Once again, Maggie wondered if her regret stemmed from drinking until she passed out. It would explain the dramatic change in her demeanor. Gone was the independent, no-nonsense woman she had met the day before. In her place was a wilted flower of a woman, given to crying spells and overwhelming fear.

"Your sister is a grown woman," Maggie said. "It wasn't your job to watch her all night. Maybe she just went back down to her cabin after some of her things."

"I don't think so. I think she was worried her husband, Jack, might show up. She acted scared when I mentioned his name."

This was new information to Maggie. "Did your sister say whether or not he was aware of their affair?"

"She never said one way or the other," Darlene said. "She just acted scared of him. Like if he knew, there would be trouble."

"If we can't get out because of the flooding and emergency services can't get in, what are the chances Charlene's husband could actually make it here?"

"I don't know," Darlene admitted. "I don't know if there's even a chance, but something was scaring my sister last night, and when I woke up this morning, she was gone. Just gone."

"If she's down by the cabins, Brett will find her." Maggie took a deep breath. "In fact, that's one of the reasons I came up here to speak with you. Brett has asked Tom to help remove Dale from the cabin. They're going to put him in a tarp and carry him up here. They want to put him in the freezer you have."

Darlene's face turned white. "In my freezer?"

"I know it's rather shocking, but you have to think about it this way, it's not cold enough outside to preserve a body for very long. Something must be done with him, and right now, the choices are very, very limited. Can you think of another place where he could be stored until the coroner is able to get through?"

"No, I suppose you're right." Darlene led Maggie outside of the cabin and into the one next door. Maggie followed her to a large kitchen. "I don't like this one bit, but I think you're right. There really isn't a better place to put him right now."

Maggie hesitated before she spoke again. She waited to see if Darlene was going to collapse into a fresh round of tears. "I'm sure my husband will arrange things so that it will be very discreet," she said, choosing her words carefully.

Darlene shuddered. "I appreciate that."

"Do you have any idea who might have wanted to hurt Dale?" Maggie asked. "Aside from maybe Charlene's husband. What did you say his name was?"

"Jack, Jack Reed," Darlene said. "And no, I can't think of anyone who would want to hurt him. Despite all of this, Dale was a decent man. Believe it or not, he did love his wife, but he also loved my sister. I won't pretend to understand their relationship, but it just went on for so long that it became reality and no longer a question. Do you know what I mean?"

"Not really," Maggie said. "Unless you just mean that you stopped asking questions about it after so many years."

Darlene smiled and nodded. "That's exactly what I mean. After a while, their affair just became part of the dynamic of our family. Charlene had Jack, and she also had Dale."

Maggie heard footsteps on the front porch. She assumed it was Brett and Tom with Dale's body. "Why don't we go have a seat on the other side of the house?" she suggested. Darlene nodded and seemed to understand her intention. She led her back through the long hallway and into a sitting room in the back.

"Come in," Darlene called out when she heard a knock on the door. Maggie hoped the guys heard her well enough that they could just remain where they were while they carried Dale's body across the house to the other side. She didn't want to see the tarp herself, and she was quite sure Darlene didn't need to see it, either.

They heard footsteps in the hallway. Maggie raised her head, suddenly aware that there was only one person walking toward them. A man appeared in the doorway, dressed in a dark green rain slicker. Reddish brown mud covered his clothing.

"Where is she, Darlene?" the man's voice boomed. "Where is my wife?"

Maggie stood up immediately. She stepped in

front of the older woman and folded her arms. "You must be Jack," she said.

"And just who do you think you are?" Jack demanded. Mud and water puddled at his feet where he stood in the doorway to the small sitting room.

"My name is Maggie and I'm a guest here. My husband is a sheriff from back home in Missouri. He is dealing with the death of another guest, but I have a feeling you already know about that."

"I don't know what you're implying, lady," Jack said. "Since you seem to know about everything, where is my wife? Where is Charlene?"

"She was gone when I got up this morning," Darlene cried. She hung her head and wiped the fresh tears from her cheeks. "What are you doing here?"

"Better yet," Maggie said. "How did you get here? As far as we know all the roads in to the campground are closed due to flooding."

"I'm still not getting any answers from the two of you," Jack said. "Where is my wife? Darlene, you better tell me where she went right now."

"Or what?" Maggie asked. "That sure sounds a lot like a threat to me."

The man stared hard at her for a moment. "No, ma'am. No, that wasn't a threat," he said. "I'm telling you straight out, there's going to be trouble if I don't get answers about my wife. And soon."

"I think Darlene told you already," Maggie said. "Charlene was gone when she got up this morning. I just came up here from my own cabin and I haven't seen her either. Neither of us know where she is."

"You'd better hope I find her." Jack turned around and stomped back down the hall.

CHAPTER NINE

After Jack left, Maggie immediately went to Darlene's side. "What was that all about?"

"That's not good news," Darlene said.

"Do you think he's capable of hurting anyone?"

Darlene quickly wiped her eyes before a fresh barrage of tears could overtake her. "I'm so worried about my sister," she wailed.

"Do you think Jack could hurt someone?" Maggie asked.

"I just don't know."

Maggie heard the sound of someone at the back door. "Please let that be Brett." She patted Darlene's hand and stood up. "I'm going to check and see if that's my husband. You stay right here, okay?"

Darlene nodded. "I am so worried about my sister," she repeated.

Maggie rushed out of the room and down the hall toward the back door. When she pulled the door open, she was face to face with Brett. His arms were wrapped around one end of the tarp while Tom carried the other end. She rushed back to the sitting room and stood in the doorway to prevent Darlene from seeing the body. "Wait here, Darlene," she said.

She waited until she heard Brett thank Tom for his help before she moved from the door.

"I don't know if this is appropriate to say, but we have a problem." Maggie wished she could handle things alone but knew that wasn't practical. Brett needed to know what was going on as soon as possible.

"What's going on?" Brett asked. "You look like you've seen a ghost."

"That's ironic," Tom said.

"Listen to me," Maggie said. "I don't know how much time I'm going to have to explain this before Darlene comes out of that room. When she woke up this morning, Charlene was gone. They were up late in the night discussing what had happened to Dale and now Darlene is beside herself with worry about her sister."

"Where did she go?" Tom asked.

"That's the thing. We have no idea. I was hopeful you'd tell me you had seen her down at the cabin where she had been staying with Dale."

"We didn't see her," Tom admitted.

"Okay, well, that's only part of the problem."

"What is the other part?" Brett asked.

"Did you see a man leaving here a few minutes ago?"

Brett looked over at Tom. "Yeah, he passed us on the way up the trail," he said. "I just assumed he was another guest of the campground. What happened?"

Maggie shook her head vigorously. "That was Jack Reed, Charlene's husband."

"Oh, no," Brett said. "That's not good news."

Tom huffed. "I hate to tell you guys this, but that wasn't Jack Reed. The man we just passed on the trail outside is not Charlene's husband. I don't know who it was, but it wasn't Jack."

Maggie looked instinctively toward the entryway sitting room. "But Darlene said that's who he was. He demanded to know where his wife was. Are you sure it wasn't him?"

"I know Jack, and that wasn't him. I've been married to my wife for more than forty years. I've known all about Dale and his extramarital activities and I'm well acquainted with Charlene, Darlene, and Jack. I don't know what is going on around here, but that wasn't him."

Without another word, Brett walked out of the kitchen and headed back down the dimly lit hallway toward the sitting room. Maggie and Tom followed close behind. Brett stepped inside the room and folded his arms over his chest. "Darlene, who was that that just left here?" he asked. "I know that wasn't your brother-in-law."

"Brett, she's not here," Maggie said.

"Sure, she is." Brett crossed the floor to the over-sized chair where Darlene had been seated. He moved back a stack of blankets and pillows to reveal an empty seat. "I thought she was just resting. I thought she was right there."

"Where did she go?" Maggie moved around the room and looked for any sign of the woman. "I didn't even hear the door shut."

"Wonderful," Brett said. "Now we have two missing women and a stranger passing himself off as the husband of the one having an affair."

"What are we going to do now?" Tom asked.

"Right now, I want you to go back to your cabin with your wife," Brett said. "Stay inside with the doors locked and don't open them for anyone but me or Maggie. I'm going to try and see if I can get the police on the phone. This is starting to get out of hand."

"Do you think my wife is in danger?" Tom asked.

"It's possible," Brett said.

Tom said nothing more. He rushed out of the room and down the hall. Maggie heard the door slam behind him and turned to Brett. "Do you really think someone might hurt Sadie?"

"I don't know, but I definitely can't rule it out," he said. "We need to find Darlene and her sister."

"And whoever that was claiming to be her husband," Maggie added. She signed. "Why would Darlene lie about her brother-in-law?"

"I have no idea," he said. "I am as confused as I was the moment Charlene pounded on our cabin door. Honestly, honey, my instincts are all over the place with this case."

"What do you want to do now?" Maggie asked.

"The first thing I want to do is try the phone in the other room," Brett said. "Who knows? Maybe we'll get lucky and actually reach the police this time."

"Right, yeah," Maggie said. "That's a really good idea."

He found the phone immediately and pulled it away from the wall. He turned the speaker on and dialed 911. At first, all they heard was static. "Come on, come on," Brett said.

"Just give it a second," Maggie whispered, crossing her fingers behind her back.

The static on the other end increased for a second, and then they heard a dial tone. "Gerard County," a voice on the other end said, followed by gibberish.

"Hello, hello!" Brett shouted into the phone. "We're out here at the Sleepy Pines Campground, located off of Hwy. 121. There has been a murder. I repeat, a murder has taken place. Please send law enforcement as soon as possible."

They waited together for a response. "Hello, hello," Brett said again. Seconds later, a new wave of static erupted on the other end of the line. The static was followed by dead silence.

"Try them again," Maggie suggested. Brett hung up the phone and dialed the emergency line one more time. This time, they heard nothing but silence. "I'll stay here and keep trying. I think you need to go look for Darlene and her sister. I have no idea who that man was, but I have a feeling we're all in danger."

"I think you're right," Brett said. "Which exactly why I am not leaving you here. You're coming with me. We're going to go cabin to cabin and check with everyone to see if they have heard or seen anything."

"Are you sure?"

"I'm absolutely sure that I'm not going to let you out of my sight."

CHAPTER TEN

Brett started with cabin number one. He pounded on the door and waited for someone to answer. When no one came, he peered in the front windows. "It's dark in there," he said. "I don't think anyone is staying in this one."

"I can see a light shining in the kitchen of the one next door," Maggie said. They stepped off the porch and rushed across the way to the next cabin. Brett knocked on the door.

A young-looking man with long hair gathered in a ponytail answered the door. "Can I help you?"

"I don't have time to explain everything right now, but I'm a law enforcement officer. One of the guests has passed away and we are looking for the owner of this place. Have you seen Darlene? She would be the woman who checked you in when you arrived."

The young man shook his head. He stepped back from the front door and opened it wide enough for them to see inside. "It's just my wife and me," he said. "The last time I saw Darlene, she knocked on our door to let us know about the flooding. Is everything okay, man?"

"I don't know, to be honest," Brett said. "Listen, keep your wife inside and stay with her. Do not answer the door for anyone you don't know. We've tried to place a call to the police but I'm not sure it went through."

"I thought you said you were the police," the man said, pushing the door closed a little.

"I am, but I'm here on vacation, too." Brett pulled his badge out of his back pocket and showed it to the man. "You'll see that it says Dogwood Mountain County, Missouri. That's where I'm a county sheriff. Stay inside, please. I mean it."

The young man shut the door quickly. Maggie could hear the lock turn as soon as the door was closed. "What now?"

"Now we make our way down the row toward our own cabin." Brett walked back out into the rain and stepped up onto the next porch. The next two cabins were empty. The scene replayed itself three more times before they reached the Johnsons' cabin.

"Should we check on Tom and Sadie?" Maggie asked.

"I think we should give them an update." Brett walked across the front porch and knocked. Tom pulled the door open a second later and came outside.

"What's going on now?" His hand gripped the doorknob even after he shut the door behind them.

"Nothing new," Brett said. "Have you seen anyone? The sisters or the man claiming to be Jack Reed?"

Tom shook his head. "No, I haven't seen anyone," he said. "We're staying inside just like you told us to."

"How is Sadie doing?"

Tom looked over his shoulder. "She's still resting. I haven't told her anything about seeing the man claiming to be Charlene's husband. I don't want to upset her any more than she already is."

"Is everything okay in there?" Brett asked.

Tom looked back again and shook his head. "Everything is fine," he said with a strained chuckle. "I'm just worried about my wife. She's not acting like herself. I'm afraid all of this anxiety over her step-brother's death is really getting to her."

"Do you want me to take a look at her? I do have some medical training," Brett said. "I'm trained in CPR."

Tom shook his head and smiled. "No, that isn't necessary. I don't think she's on the brink of a medical emergency or anything. She's just under a lot of stress and strain. I don't want to increase that."

"Alright." Brett nodded. "Just so you know, I think we got a hold of the police. I hope we see lights and sirens here shortly." He took Maggie by the hand and pulled her off the front porch after they said goodbye. They walked quickly to the front porch of their own cabin.

"Why did you tell him that?" Maggie asked when they were far enough away. "Why did you tell him the police were on their way when we don't know if they are?"

"I was just following my gut instincts," he said. "I don't know if anything is going on inside that cabin, but I have a feeling there's more to his story than he just told us."

"Do you think we should go back and demand to be let in?"

"I don't even have my service weapon here," Brett said. "If someone is in the cabin with them, me barging in isn't going to do anyone any good."

"So, what do we do? Just sit around here and wait?"

"I think that's all we can do," Brett said. "That and hope the police really did get my call."

Maggie jumped when thunder cracked loudly in the distance. "Maybe we should go back and look inside the empty cabins. What if someone is hiding in one of them?"

"That's not a bad idea."

"We might as well. We can't just go back to our cabin and sit and twiddle our thumbs while three people are missing. I mean, there's a good chance one of those people is the reason the other two are missing."

"We don't know that. We don't know anything for sure."

"Which is exactly why I think we should go look," Maggie said. "I know this is your line of work, but it makes sense to me that we wouldn't stop looking until we find something."

"I don't want you to take this the wrong way, but it would be completely different if I had a team of trained police officers with me. It's just you and me. We are unarmed and have no idea what we might be walking into."

"We also have no idea what we might run into

tonight if we don't do something now," Maggie said. "I've been assuming all along that Dale's death and the sisters' disappearance are all related because they're family, but what if that's not true? What if someone just targeted them randomly and they happen to share a relationship? What if there is someone out here looking to harm someone, and we might be next?"

"Let's just get out of the rain for a moment." Brett took her arm and led her past the next log cabins onto their own front porch. "Trust me, all sorts of possibilities have been running through my mind. I don't like feeling like I'm sitting here vulnerable and unable to protect you."

"Then let's go back," Maggie said. "Let's go back and just make sure that no one is holding Darlene and her sister Charlene in one of those empty cabins."

"What if we run into Jack Reed or at least the man who's pretending to be him? None of this makes any sense. I can't wrap my mind around what is really going on here."

Maggie stood in front of her husband and placed her hands on his shoulders. "Someone is lying," she said bluntly. "We have to face the fact that one of the people that we've spoken to in the last twenty-four hours is lying to us."

"I think that's sort of a given," Brett said.

"No, I mean it," she said. "Why would Darlene say the man that was in her house was her brother-in-law if he wasn't?"

"Why would Tom say the man wasn't who Darlene said he was if he wasn't?" Brett said.

Maggie smiled. "Exactly. We need to start over from the beginning and get to the bottom of this before someone else ends up dead." She stepped back inside their cabin for a moment, wanting to put on a dry pair of socks and another layer of clothing. The sun had already begun to go down and the air outside took on a colder chill than the night before. The rain continued to fall in sheets.

While she changed, Brett scoured the inside of the cabin for anything that might help them in their search. Maggie pulled a sweatshirt over her head and went into the kitchen. She cobbled together a couple of sandwiches and wrapped them in plastic, then stuffed them into the pouch of her sweatshirt for later.

"Ready?" Brett asked her when they stood by the front door.

"As ready as I'm ever going to be." Maggie took Brett by the hand and led him through the front door. They trudged slowly back up the hill toward the first empty cabin. Brett boldly stepped up on the front porch and twisted the doorknob, surprised when the door opened.

"Hello? Is anyone in here?" Brett called into the empty and dark room. Maggie flipped on the light switch near the front door and waited there while Brett made his way through the small cabin. "Nothing."

"One down, four more to go," Maggie said. They stepped off the porch together and headed to the next empty cabin. Maggie kept watch again as Brett made his way through each one.

They walked together to the last cabin. "I don't think we're going to find anything in this one, either," Brett said. "There wasn't even a trace left behind that someone had been in any of these cabins."

"We're missing something," Maggie said. "I can feel it." She waited while Brett forced the front door of the last cabin open and stepped inside. He turned the light on himself this time and walked slowly through each room. The wind picked up outside and Maggie went inside the front room herself, holding the door with her free hand. She waited for Brett to rejoin her in the living room.

Outside the living room window, she caught a glimpse of something moving. With her hands still on the doorknob, she moved to the large window and peered outside. Tom appeared with Sadie by his side, both carrying several pieces of luggage. They were walking up the path toward the entrance of the campground. Maggie watched as Sadie looked around in all directions, as if she was waiting for someone.

"What's going on?" Brett said when he reentered the living room. Maggie held her finger to her lips and motioned for him to come and join her at the window. "Where are they going?"

"That's what I'd like to know," Maggie said.

CHAPTER ELEVEN

Before the Johnsons could reach the top of the hill, sirens wailed in the distance. Maggie took one look at Brett and headed out the front door. He pulled the door shut quietly behind him and waited on the front porch.

They watched as the Johnsons stopped moving. Tom took a bag from his wife and slung it over his own shoulder then hooked his arm in hers and led her to the space between the first and second cabin. Maggie looked up at Brett. "I think I know what's going on," she said.

"What do you mean?" Brett whispered.

"Just follow me," Maggie said quietly. "I have a feeling I know where Darlene and her sister are." She cast another look back up the hill before she stepped off the porch. Her heart raced and she hoped it wasn't too late.

"Where are we going?" Brett asked as she dragged him along in the rain.

"Back to the Johnsons' cabin," Maggie said. "If we're lucky, we'll find Darlene and Charlene in there alive."

"Wait a minute," Brett said. He stopped and turned her around to look at him. "You think the Johnsons have Darlene and Charlene?"

"I don't think they're the Johnsons at all," Maggie said. "As a matter of fact, I'm pretty sure Sadie isn't Dale's stepsister at all."

"You're saying you think it was all a lie?"

Maggie shook her head. "Not all of it," she said. "I'm sure they were telling the truth about the relationship between Charlene, Darlene, and Dale, but I also think it's very likely that Tom is the killer."

Brett took the umbrella from her and led her quickly back down the hill. They stopped in front of Tom and Sadie's cabin. Maggie felt her heart sink to her stomach when she spotted an orange glow from inside the living room window. "Brett! The cabin is on fire." She threw the umbrella down on the porch and raced to the front door.

"Stay back!" Brett stepped to the edge of the

porch and ran towards the door, pushing into it with his shoulder. The door gave and he landed in the middle of the living room. Maggie rushed in behind him and helped him to his feet. "The utility room!"

Maggie peeled her sweatshirt off and wrapped it around her head, covering her mouth. Brett caught her by the shoulder. "Run outside. Run to the back door and try to get it open." She immediately headed through the living room.

The next few moments flew by. Maggie found herself at the back door, yanking hard on the doorknob. As soon as the door gave, she found herself on her rear end in the mud. She scrambled quickly to her feet and ran inside the open door.

Charlene lay unconscious next to her sister. Both women were bound and gagged. Brett burst into the room a second later. He untied Charlene's ankles and helped her to her feet then passed her off to Maggie, who led her gently outside while Brett returned to help Darlene.

Charlene opened her eyes as soon as the rain began to hit her face. Her eyes were wild, and she backed up several feet. "I know you're scared, but we're here to help. The Johnsons left you and your sister alone in the cabin." She held her hands up and slowly approached the bound woman, pulling the gag away from her mouth and quickly undoing her wrists.

"My sister," Charlene cried. "They have my sister, too."

"Help me," Brett said. He was still holding Darlene up. Her eyes were closed.

"Oh, Darlene," Charlene cried. She rushed to her sister's side and began untying the ropes around her wrists and ankles. Maggie patted the woman's face vigorously. She breathed the sigh of relief when Darlene's eyes popped open and focused on her sister.

"Who did this to you?" Brett demanded. He stood in front of both women. "I need you to be very clear with me, right now. The police are on their way. Who did this to you?"

"I don't know who they were," Charlene said. "It was the older man and woman who were in this cabin. They showed up at Darlene's last night and threatened me. They said they would hurt my sister if I didn't come with them."

"Did they say anything else? Do you know what they wanted with you?" Brett asked.

Charlene shook her head. "I only heard them talking about a couple of people who were meddling in their plan. They were talking about what to do and the man said it was too risky to get rid of the couple. I honestly thought they were watching a movie or something."

"My head hurts," Darlene said. "I feel like I'm swimming."

"I think my sister has been drugged," Charlene said. "She's not acting like herself. When they brought her back into the cabin with me, she acted like she was half asleep already."

Brett turned to Darlene. "Can you remember anything?" he asked. "Anything at all about how you got here?"

Darlene seemed to wobble on her feet. Charlene caught her before she fell over again. "Oh, no. Jack is here! I saw him."

"Charlene, is it possible that your husband is here?" Brett asked.

Charlene blinked "I don't know how, but maybe."

"Are you sure that was your brother-in-law?" Maggie asked.

Darlene's eyes focused on Maggie. "Yes, I'm sure," she said, looking at her sister. "I didn't tell him anything about who you were here with. You must believe me."

"She's telling the truth," a man's voice said behind them. Maggie turned around quickly and spotted the man who had threatened her a short time before in Darlene's house. It was Jack Reed, or at least the man Darlene had identified as Jack.

"I need you to stay back there, buddy," Brett said. He stepped out in front of the women. "I don't know who you really are, but the police are on their way."

"My name is Jack Reed," he said. "That woman back there is my wife. I came here to take her home."

"How did you get here?" Maggie asked. "The roads are all flooded."

Jack smiled. "Let's just say this country boy knows his way around the back roads."

"You still haven't told us why you came," Charlene said. "Why are you here, Jack? After all of these years, why show up now?"

"I wouldn't have been here at all if that woman hadn't called me," Jack said.

"What woman?" Brett asked him.

"I don't know her name, but she said she was married to Dale Bushman," Jack said. Dale's name seemed to leave a bad taste in his mouth. "I've got all kinds of feelings and things to say about what's been going on between you and that man for years, Charlene. But the way she talked; I couldn't just leave you out here alone. I don't know what's been happening, but I've been trying to call you for days."

"What did this woman say to you?" Brett asked.

Jack looked around and cleared his throat. "She said she was going to end this thing between my wife and Dale, once and for all. But the way she said it left me thinking that she might have intended to do more than just show up here and break the two of them up."

"Dale was murdered last night," Brett said. "Can you account for your whereabouts in the last twenty-four hours?"

"I sure can," Jack said with a nod. "I have no problem sitting down and talking with any officer of the law about where I have been."

Maggie looked up in time to see two uniformed officers heading their way. She stayed with the sisters and Jack while Brett stepped forward and began speaking with the officers.

CHAPTER TWELVE

"I still don't get it," Orson grumbled. He was seated in front of the bonfire on Ruby's farm three nights later.

"Which part?" Brett asked.

Orson shook his head. "I just don't see how you knew that couple was lying about who they said they were," he said, looking right at Maggie. "How did you know they were the ones who killed Dale?"

Maggie inhaled deeply before she tried to answer Orson's question. It was still strange to hear the names of the people she had gotten to know so quickly. "I didn't know at first, but when Tom didn't recognize Jack, I began to get suspicious."

"Jack was the real husband of the woman who had the affair?"

Maggie nodded her head. She closed her eyes for a moment and recalled the moment when she saw the couple emerge from their hiding place, led out by a pair of officers in handcuffs.

"I didn't catch on at first, either," Brett said. "Darlene never indicated anything when we talked about the Johnsons. I would have gone right along not realizing there was something going on there if my wife here hadn't picked up on it first."

"I can't take all the credit," Maggie said. "As a matter of fact, in the beginning, I suspected Charlene was the killer. I thought it was a little suspicious that there were no tracks coming from the back of her cabin."

"Did you ever figure out what happened there?" Ruby asked.

"The minute the police arrived; the older couple known to us as the Johnsons decided to call their attorneys. I believe the running theory is that Dale's wife hired the two of them. I have a feeling there was a miscommunication somewhere and they killed the wrong person. I think Charlene was the intended target all along."

"That does make sense," Brooks said. He sat next to Myra. "If you think about it, it's likely they snuck into the cabin through the front door and hit the first person they saw."

"But when the flooding came, they ran out of options," Brett said. "I think I see where your theory is going. You think they made up the part about being related to Dale, don't you?"

Brooks nodded. "It makes sense. I bet the first thing they did was drug Darlene, and the next was to kidnap Charlene before she had a chance to tell anyone the difference."

"Which is why Darlene didn't correct anything I might have said that was wrong when I walked back up to her cabin to check on her sister," Maggie said. "I bet that's what Sadie was doing when she was supposed to be taking a nap."

"I think you're right," Brett said. "I think that's why Tom got so nervous when she started in about her childhood. She was talking too much. He was afraid she was going to spill too many details that didn't add up."

Maggie sat back in her seat and sipped the glass of wine in her hand. She was so glad to be back at home with her friends. She squeezed Brett's hand and gazed over at him.

"Here we are," Naomi sang. She walked around the circle of chairs carrying a large tray in her arms.

"What's all this?" Maggie asked.

"This is the new and improved strawberry jalapeño doughnut," Naomi said.

"The first two didn't go over very well with the customers," Ruby said with a forced smile.

"No, they didn't." Naomi lowered the tray and offered a donut to Maggie. "After the first batch, I had a hard time regulating the right amount of jalapeño juice."

"Oh, no." Maggie handed a donut over to Brett. "We're in this together, baby."

"Oh, yes, we are," Brett said, taking the donut from her. He took a large bite and sat back in his chair.

"And here we were, afraid that the effects of this disaster of a honeymoon might affect your relationship," Orson said with a smirk.

Maggie gazed at Brett. "I don't think either of us planned for things to go like they did, but it didn't hurt anything relationship wise."

"Well?" Naomi asked, nodding to the donut in Brett's hand. "What do you think about it, Sheriff?"

"I think they're excellent, and I think my wife knows how to pick the right people to work in her donut shop. These are really good, Naomi."

Maggie exhaled and took a bite. She was immediately pleased with a combination of flavors. "These are so good." She took another bite before she spoke again. "Have you guys served this version yet? Are they on the menu?"

"You just sit back in that chair and settle down," Orson said. "You're not back at work yet. Why don't you just sit there and enjoy that donut and stop trying to market it? If this little adventure taught you anything, it ought to be to stop and smell the roses once in a while."

Maggie smiled. "Point taken."

AUTHOR'S NOTE

I'd love to hear your thoughts on my books, the storylines, and anything else that you'd like to comment on—reader feedback is very important to me. My contact information, along with some other helpful links, is listed on the next page. If you'd like to be on my list of "folks to contact" with updates, release and sales notifications, etc.… just shoot me an email and let me know. Thanks for reading!

Also…

… if you're looking for more great reads, Summer Prescott Books publishes several popular series by outstanding Cozy Mystery authors.

CONTACT SUMMER PRESCOTT
BOOKS PUBLISHING

Blog and Book Catalog: http://summerprescottbooks.com

Email: summer.prescott.cozies@gmail.com

And…be sure to check out the Summer Prescott Cozy Mysteries fan page and Summer Prescott Books Publishing Page on Facebook – let's be friends!

To sign up for our fun and exciting newsletter, which will give you opportunities to win prizes and swag, enter contests, and be the first to know about New Releases, click here: http://summerprescottbooks.com

Printed in Great Britain
by Amazon